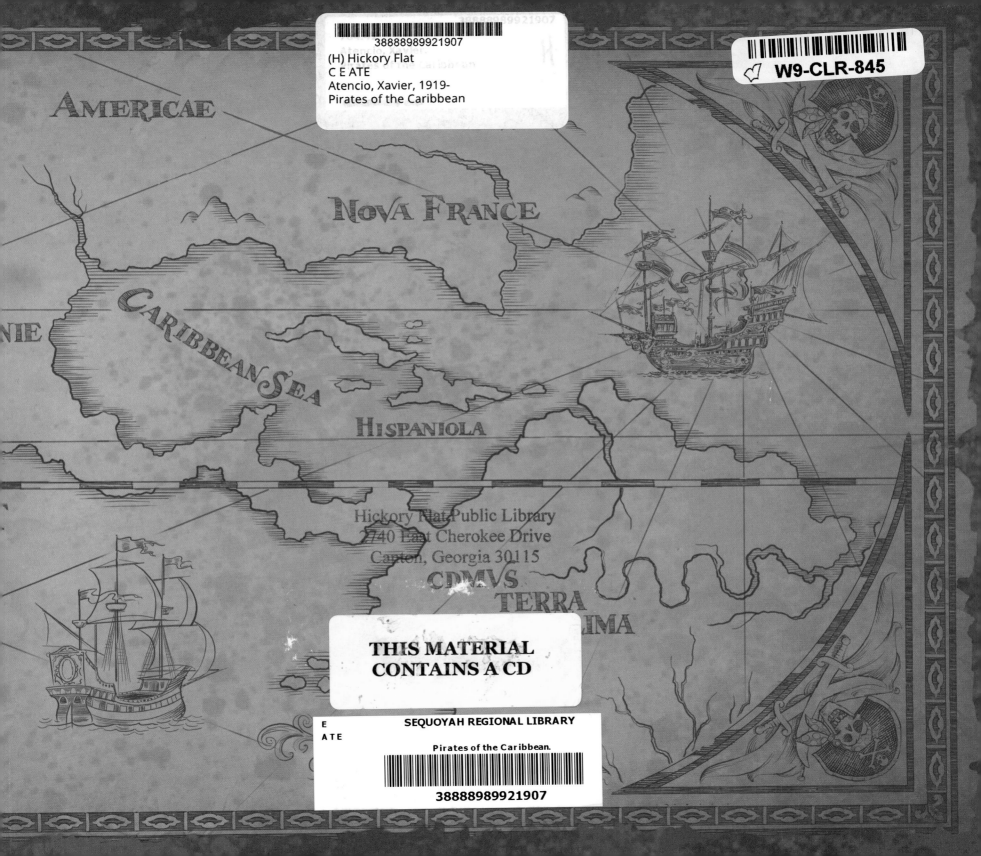

AMERICAE

NOVA FRANCE

CARIBBEAN SEA

HISPANIOLA

CDMVS
TERRA
IMA

Disney Parks

PRESENTS

Pirates
of the
Caribbean

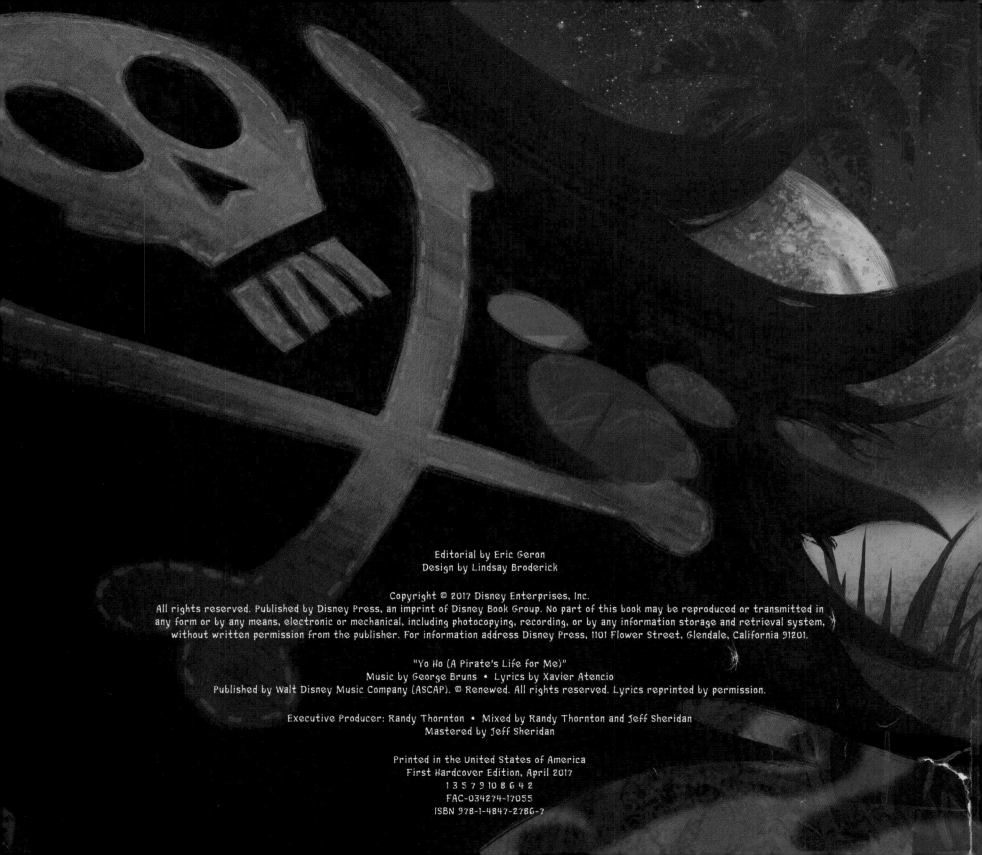

Editorial by Eric Geron
Design by Lindsay Broderick

"Yo Ho (A Pirate's Life for Me)"
Music by George Bruns • Lyrics by Xavier Atencio
Published by Walt Disney Music Company (ASCAP). © Renewed. All rights reserved. Lyrics reprinted by permission.

Executive Producer: Randy Thornton • Mixed by Randy Thornton and Jeff Sheridan
Mastered by Jeff Sheridan

Printed in the United States of America
First Hardcover Edition, April 2017
1 3 5 7 9 10 8 6 4 2
FAC-034274-17055
ISBN 978-1-4847-2786-7

Disney Parks

PRESENTS

Pirates of the CARIBBEAN

MUSIC BY **George Bruns**

LYRICS BY **Xavier Atencio**

ILLUSTRATIONS BY **Mike Wall**

Disney PRESS

Los Angeles • New York

and plundering pirates lurking in every cove!

DEAD
DEAD
DEAD MEN
MEN
DEAD MEN
TELL MEN TALES!
TELL NO TALES!
TELL NO NO
NO TALES!
TALES!

DEAD
DEAD
DEAD MEN
MEN
TELL
DEAD MEN
TELL NO TALES!
TELL
NO NO TALES!

Captain's Quarters KEEP OL

Now proceed at your own risk. . . .

a pirate's life for me!

We kidnap and ravage and don't give a hoot!
Drink up, me 'earties, YO HO!

Maraud and embezzle
and even highjack!
Drink up, me 'earties, YO HO!

We kindle and char, inflame and ignite!
Drink up, me 'earties, YO HO!

We're rascals, scoundrels, villains, and knaves! Drink up, me 'earties, YO HO!

We're devils and black sheep,
we're really **bad** eggs.
Drink up, me 'earties, YO HO!

Yo ho, yo ho,
a pirate's life for me!

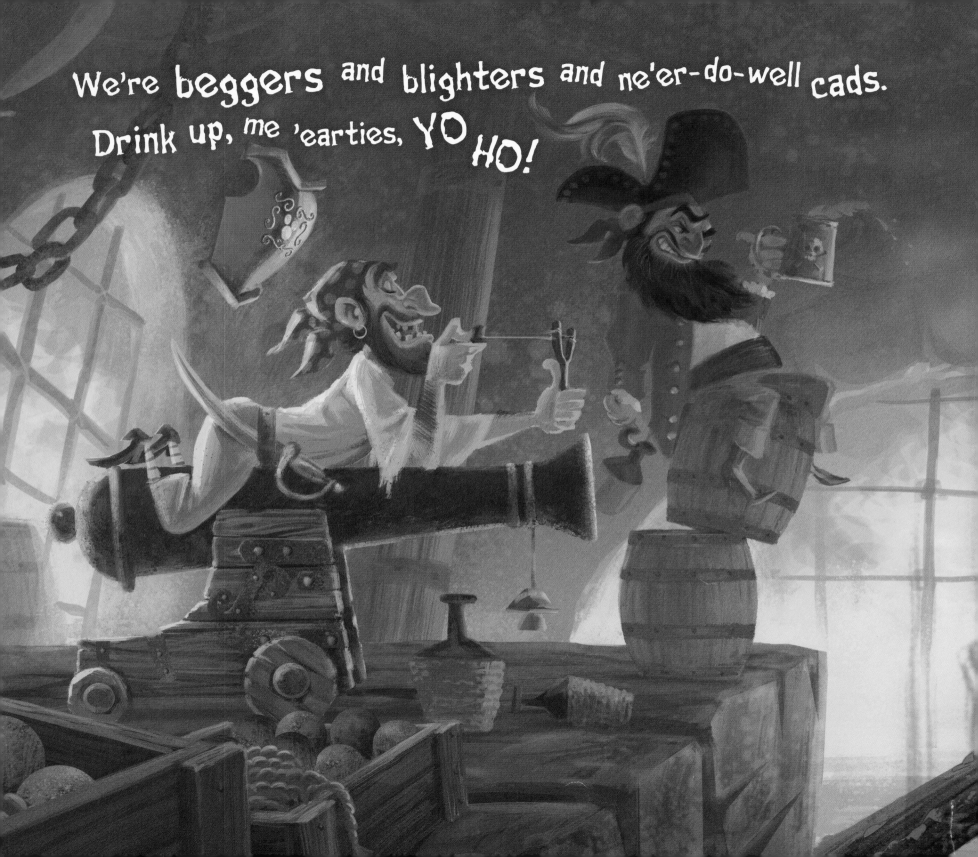

Aye, but we're **loved** by our mommies 'n' dads.
Drink up, me 'earties, YO HO!

PIRATES of the CARIBBEAN

NOVA
HIS

EQVINOC